the
TREE
and
FOUR FRIENDS

Words and Pictures by Aline Cunningham

Copyright © 1975 Concordia Publishing House
ISBN 0-570-06908-4

I like to climb the big oak tree. No one
knows I am there.

I like to swing on my swing.

We like to play under the big oak tree.
It is cool there on a warm summer day.

We build our nest in the big oak tree.
We are happy there.

Our babies like the big oak tree too.

I sing beautiful songs for everyone.

I like to store nuts and acorns in the big oak tree.

My family lives up at the top.

In the winter we sleep in a hole in the trunk, all cozy and warm.

At first I am very tiny. I am a katydid.

My friends and I grow up in the big oak tree.

We sing each warm summer night.

"Katy-did! Katy-did!"

We sing the song of summer.

The tree is a gift from God.
We all share it.